DJ LIL JAY

WRITTEN BY: Superstar Jay
WITH: Heddrick McBride
ILLUSTRATED BY: HH-Pax

Copyright © 2022 McBride Collection of Stories
All rights reserved.

ISBN: 978-1-7361082-8-4

Dedication

I dedicate this book to my grandmother, Vera Hamilton, my daughter, Jaylah Hamilton, and my family and friends. Without their support and belief in me, there wouldn't be a Superstar Jay. So my advice to the world is to show up, don't quit, and appreciate your blessings.

4

CHAPTER ONE
AN EXCITING VISITOR

One Friday afternoon, Michael ran straight home from school without stopping. He passed the barbershop, the supermarket, and all of the houses on his street. He finally ended up in his living room.

"Good afternoon, mom. Is he here?" Michael asked as he hung his bag in the closet where jackets were kept. Throughout his day at school, Michael had been waiting for each minute to pass before he could go back home and see his visitor. Michael was so excited he could barely sit still in class, let alone pay complete attention to his teacher. His mind always focused on his home and the guest he was to have that day. His mom had said that she would stay home today from work and prepare for his arrival. Michael rushed upstairs to his room from the hallway and changed his clothes.

It was a Friday, so he would have a lot of time to do his homework.

He was so happy that he almost bumped into the dining room table when he saw the visitor, his uncle.

"Uncle Jay!" Michael shouted with happiness.

Uncle Jay was a tall, athletic man that Michael loved so much. He visited once every month because he lived so far away. Uncle Jay loved to smile and make others smile too. He loved to make people laugh by telling silly jokes and giving them gifts.

"Mikey! You have grown so big now!" Uncle Jay said with a big smile, hugging his nephew, who ran and jumped into his arms.

"You've grown too, Uncle Jay!" Michael said smiling. Michael loved to smile, just like his uncle.

"I waited for you all day at school," Michael said excitedly as his uncle set him down on a chair at the table.

"And I was right here waiting for you!" Uncle Jay said, sitting right down beside him.

Michael's mother walked out of the kitchen with a big batch of brownies and a jug of milk. She also had dark chocolate skin and dark brown eyes that shone each time she smiled. She wore a yellow dress that made her skin glow. On her head, she had long braids that she made into a big bun on the top of her head.

   After finishing their snacks and walking back into the kitchen, Michael and his Uncle Jay began to talk.

14

CHAPTER TWO
THE DJ

It was cold but Michael and his uncle sat outside on the front doorsteps just enjoying a good talk.

"Uncle Jay, how is Aunty Jay?" Michael kindly asked.

"Your Aunty Jay is doing just fine. She misses you, and that's why she sent those toys that I gave you earlier today," Uncle Jay said with a wide smile.

"Thank you, Aunty Jay!" Michael said happily. "There is one question I want to ask you, Uncle Jay. I have been thinking about it all week!"

"Ask away, Mikey."

"Could you tell me all about your career as a DJ?" Mikey asked.

Now, that was one unique thing about Uncle Jay. He was the most famous DJ in the country. He loved music as much as he loved helping other people. He loved music since he was a child, and he told Michael all about using music to keep everyone happy.

He had a famous name. Everyone called him DJ Lil Jay.

Michael would hang out with Uncle Jay at his music studio while Uncle Jay played his favorite songs. When his uncle went out to perform at concerts, Michael would watch videos of Uncle Jay playing music on what he called a mixer and turntables.

"Hmm," Uncle Jay said.

"How would you like me to tell you all about how I became a DJ?"

Michael was so excited, he smiled extra wide and couldn't say a word.

Uncle Jay gave a big laugh and started his story.

22

CHAPTER THREE
THE STORY OF LIL JAY

When Uncle Jay was still a young boy, everyone called him 'Little Jay.' He loved to listen to his daddy's record player and watch music videos on the old TV that sat in the living room. Little Jay was as little as his name, and his favorite DJ was Dr. Dre, who was still a popular teenager at that time. So, when listening to Dr. Dre on the turntable, Little Jay would always wonder how all those different kinds of music blended so perfectly.

   Little Jay knew he loved music so much that he wanted to become a DJ when he grew up. Back then, Little Jay's mama always told him that he wasn't too little to do anything. He believed it and began to learn more about music. Even at age 12, Little Jay knew that he would have to work extremely hard to be the best DJ in the world, just like his role model.

   Little Jay lived in a small town where everyone knew their neighbors.

There was one special neighbor named Jaylah that Little Jay loved to visit. Little Jay loved these visits because she loved music as much as he did. Jaylah was an excellent singer, and everyone enjoyed hearing her voice. When Little Jay heard her sing, he started to call her 'Superstar Jaylah.' After all, she was a superstar to him.

She had light brown skin and long, thick curly hair. And that voice! It sounded like a priceless musical instrument. She was tall and beautiful and loved to help Little Jay's mom bake. "Superstar Jaylah" even brought many records over for Little Jay to play, expanding his musical horizons.

Uncle Jay could remember feeling nervous and a little shaky on his first day in his new school.

He thought he could make a great first impression if he dressed up in his favorite clothes and shoes.

His mother walked him to school just so he could settle down. Little Jay then thought everything was going to be just fine.

But he was a little bit wrong.

It all started happening when he walked into his first-class of the day. A boy called Dennis with fair skin and short blonde hair that touched his ears was a little taller than Little Jay. He had bright blue eyes and wore a white shirt and a pair of blue shorts that day.

"What are you wearing? It's your first day of school. You are dressed like it's Halloween!" The boy said loudly, and a lot of other boys joined in.

After that, Little Jay knew that maybe it wouldn't be the best first day of school after all.

30

CHAPTER FOUR
LITTLE JAY WORKS HARD.

His fellow classmates laughed at Little Jay because of what he wore. When the teacher came in and asked for his name, he told the class proudly that his name was 'Little Jay.' Some children, including Dennis, laughed at his name, calling him a baby.

In his last class of the day, when the teacher called on each child to talk about dreams for the future, Little Jay was filled with excitement. He was sure that his classmates would think that his career choice was incredible and they would start to like him.

However, when he stood at the front of the class and said: "My mama has always told me that if I believed in myself and dream every day and night of being someone in the future, I would eventually be that person, successful and all!" The teacher smiled at him when he started his speech. "Well, my dream is to be a DJ when I grow up. To play great music and make a lot of people happy."

    The class was silent at first because no one saw that coming. No one laughed or teased Little Jay. They just stared at him, wondering why he hadn't chosen to become a doctor, lawyer, or a teacher.

    A girl named Mindy spoke up. She was a light-skinned girl with long brown hair that touched her waist. Her eyes were a beautiful green, and her lips were naturally pink.

"You don't look like a famous DJ." The girl shook her head.

One day, Little Jay's teacher came in with Mindy's mother.

Mindy stood up to go to the front of the class to stand beside her mom.

The teacher told the class that Mindy would have a birthday party on Saturday. Everyone was excited, including Little Jay. Superstar Jaylah was going to sing at the party.

Little Jay had a great idea! He could DJ at Mindy's party; he wasn't afraid to tell everyone!

But when they all heard his idea, they doubted whether he could do it. Mindy said she did not want her party to have boring music.

Little Jay could not believe how sad he was.

He had always gone with Superstar Jaylah to the studio and worked with her on creating music. She was the only friend who believed in him and thought he would be great. She taught him how to use the specialized DJ equipment, called turntables and mixers, to make music sing. She told him he made great music just last week when they walked back from the studio. But here he was; his own classmates didn't believe in him.

38

CHAPTER FIVE
DJ LIL JAY

When Jay arrived at the birthday party, he had a lot of fun, eating and dancing. Superstar Jaylah made sure all the kids had a great time. She wore a glittering dress, and her braids fell down her back. She wore shiny boots that made her look taller. She sang with all her heart, and everyone thought she was totally perfect.

Little Jay thought it would have been great to be the DJ at the party. But he didn't worry too much. He spoke with Superstar Jaylah and his mama about how he about his classmates not believing in his dreams. His mama and best friend were there for him. They said he didn't have to ask for other people's permission to be his best. He just had to be himself!

He didn't have to mope because people didn't think his dreams could be achieved. He just had to work even harder to make sure that dream happened. He didn't have to worry about the color of his skin or how much money he had to be a great DJ. He just had to stick with the people who loved him.

DJ Little Jay kept working hard at the studio with Superstar Jaylah. In fact, he became so focused that he went with her every weekend, and one day, he met Dr. Dre, his role model!

Meeting with Dr. Dre only made him try harder. He learned the complex parts of being a DJ and perfected them. After a few years of working with all he had, everyone who knew Little Jay, although he wasn't so little anymore, knew he excelled at music.

One day, in the music room at school, the music teacher took them all to pick out instruments. Then, without thinking, Little Jay walked to the turntable and started to spin some good tunes. Everyone in the class, even the music teacher, was shocked that he could perform so well at such a young age.

He was so good that he was chosen to be the DJ for the school dance!

He was the happiest boy in the world when that day arrived.

He walked to the DJ stand that was only designed for the DJ and rocked the school.

After that day, Little Jay went home and told his mama about his excellent school. She just laughed and told him:

"Remember the first day of school when you dressed like a DJ? No one thought you could do much. Now, the whole school and even the town know you play great music. I am so proud of you, Lil Jay."

And that was the start of his career.

Lil Jay was his DJ name from then on. DJ Lil Jay played with many bands, at concerts, and even with Dr. Dre. He was a speaker at many schools where he told the children and teens that they would go further than expected when they held on to their dreams.

VISIT
www.mcbridestories.com

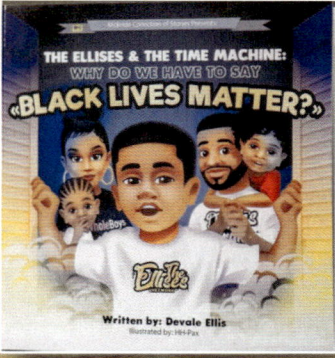

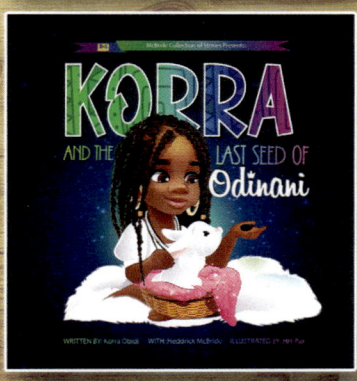
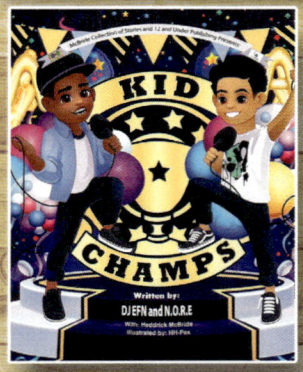

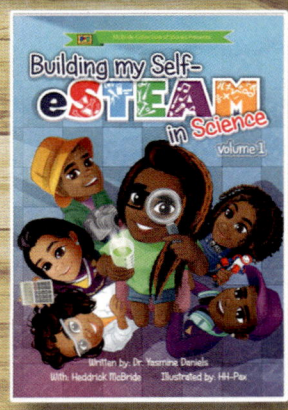
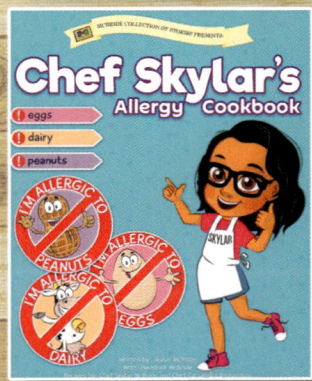

Made in the USA
Middletown, DE
02 December 2024